Information for Parents and Carers of Young Children

This book deals with the subject of a pet dying, but it is also an adventure story which is intended to be read at anytime, not just when a pet has died. Gracie's Forest Adventure explores the emotions associated with grief from a safe distance, in a fantasy world. As well as children being able to follow Gracie's adventure, the story helps children to develop an understanding of the fact that circumstances change and things happen in life. It should also help them to be empathetic to friends who are facing difficult situations.

The story is about a little girl with a magical hat that transports herself and her friends into a forest full of animated, lively characters. There are opportunities in the book for parents and carers to pause and discuss relevant situations where appropriate.

To Andrea,

Gracie's Forest Adventure

Carole Cafferty

Carole Cafferty

Matador
9 Priory Business Park,
Wistow Road, Kibworth Beauchamp,
Leicestershire. LE8 0RX
Tel: 0116 279 2299
Email: books@troubador.co.uk
Web: www.troubador.co.uk/matador
Twitter: @matadorbooks

ISBN 978 1800464 308

British Library Cataloguing in Publication Data.
A catalogue record for this book is available from the British Library.

Typeset in 17pt Blambot FXPro Light by Troubador Publishing Ltd, Leicester, UK

Matador is an imprint of Troubador Publishing Ltd

With thanks to Paula Darker and Andrea Gillibrand from Vets 4 Pets;
your help and advice in writing this book has been invaluable.

Thank you also to the children, parents and early years professionals
who have advised and supported me throughout.

It was a sunny day in Hedgehog Crescent as Gracie skipped to her friends' house to play. Arin, Bala (his little sister) and Gracie loved to go into the summer house at the bottom of the garden. Purrfect, Arin's ginger cat, sometimes liked to join in the fun too.

The children's favourite game was dressing up. They had a secret too; Gracie had a magic hat which took her and her friends on adventures into different places.

Gracie rang the door bell. Arin, Bala and their mummy opened the door.
They looked as if they had been crying and Bala was cuddling her toy rabbit.

There was something very wrong.

"Purrfect is dead!" announced Arin, dabbing his eyes with a tissue.
"He didn't eat his supper last night and it was his favourite fish."

"And he didn't want to play either," added Bala.

Mummy explained that she had taken Purrfect to Mr Badger, the vet, that
morning. The vet had examined him and given him a scan. The scan showed that
Purrfect had a very poorly tummy which could not be made better.

The only thing the vet could do to help was to give him an injection.
This stopped the pain and let Purrfect die without his tummy hurting him anymore.

The children were all upset so Arin and Bala's mummy suggested that they
should play in the garden for a while. The three of them ran through the garden,
behind the tree and into the summer house.

Purrfect's basket sat empty in the corner. "It is sad seeing Purrfect's basket empty," said Arin as he remembered Purrfect playing in the garden chasing butterflies. Gracie felt sad too. She remembered stroking the little cat's soft ginger fur.

The children looked at the rack of dressing up clothes, wondering what game to play. Gracie pulled on an explorer's cloak and passed a backpack to Bala and a telescope to Arin.

But the children felt too sad to play so they huddled together.

Then Gracie pulled on her magic hat. The children closed their eyes.

"I wish, I wish, I wish that we could all go on an adventure" she said.

The children opened their eyes; the sun was shining
and they were in a deep forest, sitting under a tree.

A little purple rabbit hopped by.
"Have you seen Hedgehog today?" asked Rabbit

"No," called the children.

There was a scratching noise. Gracie, Arin and Bala looked around;
up popped a little mole. "Have you seen Badger today?" asked Mole.

"No," called the children.

Something was happening in the forest. The
children thought it would be a good adventure
to follow Rabbit and Mole and see what it was,
so they set off, following their trail.

"Look!" squealed Bala, pointing. "A fox!"

"I hope he doesn't see Rabbit," whispered Gracie. "Foxes are sometimes dangerous for little animals."

The three children followed the little animals over a brook and into a field full of daisies and big oak trees.

From one of the trees came the sound of crying. Quietly they all peered into the hollow of the tree.

Inside was a small gathering of woodland animals.

Two little Squirrels were crying. Owl, Robin and Hedgehog watched while Badger, the vet, packed his medicines into his bag.

Just then Mole and Rabbit popped into the tree trunk. "What's wrong?" they asked.

"Squirrel Bushytail is dead!" cried the two little Squirrels.

"BushyTail was exploring in the forest and a branch fell on his head," explained Badger. "I couldn't make him better; his head was hurt too badly".

"Is he dead then?" cried one of the little Squirrels.

Owl nodded. She gathered the little animals around her.

"This is the way of life," explained Owl. "Think about daisies.
They grow from tiny seeds into beautiful flowers, but when they come
to the end of their life cycle they die and go back in to the earth.
Some die early because things can happen to them; they might get
trodden on by accident or they might not get enough sunshine.

Animals have a life cycle too; sometimes they come to the end
of their life cycle but sometimes they get ill or have an accident
and sometimes bigger animals might hurt them."

"How could this happen to Bushytail?" said Hedgehog in an angry voice.
"I thought a vet could make any animal better."

"I couldn't make Bushytail better this time," Badger explained, "so the kindest thing I could do was to stop his head hurting and let him die without pain."

Owl added: "We can't always save animals from dying. Badger did his best."

"I don't want to talk about this anymore," said Mole, as he began to dig a hole.

"We need to say goodbye to Bushytail," said the Squirrels.

"But we can still see him!" Rabbit cried.

Badger explained that when animals die, their body is still there but it doesn't work anymore. "It is a bit like a snail," he said. "When it is alive, it carries its shell around the garden and when it dies it leaves an empty shell behind."

Robin said, "It makes us very sad to say goodbye but we need to remember all the fun we had with Bushytail when we played with him in the forest."

"Shall we bury him in a nice spot or should we ask Badger to cremate him?" asked Owl.

"What does cremate mean?" asked Robin.

"It means that their body is changed to ashes. Vets do this," Owl replied.

The animals decided that under the oak tree would be a
nice place to bury Bushytail. Badger quickly started digging a
hole with his big claws. Gracie gave her cloak to the little Squirrels.
They wrapped it around Bushytail and laid him by the tree.
All the little animals gathered around to say goodbye;
even Mole popped up.

Rabbit had brought some daisy seeds for all the animals
to sprinkle at the bottom of the tree. This would make a lovely
spot for the woodland animals to remember Bushytail.

Suddenly... there was rustling behind a bush.
Everyone stopped to listen.

Gracie peeked out; she could just see the tail of Fox.
"Quick!" she called, "Hide, little animals, Fox is on the prowl".

The animals scampered away into the forest and the
children hid quietly behind the big oak as Fox slinked by.

The sun began to set and the forest started to get dark; Bala began to cry.

"What's that I can hear?" whispered Arin. The children listened.

They could hear Arin and Bala's mummy calling, "Where are you?"

The children were surprised to find themselves back in the summer house.

Quickly they ran out into the garden round the tree and nearly bumped into Arin and Bala's mummy. She had a pot in her hand. "This has Purrfect's ashes in it," she said. "Where would you like to bury him?"

Arin and Bala decided that the corner of the garden where the daisies grew would be a nice place because Purrfect often sat there watching the butterflies.

The children gathered round as Mummy buried Purrfect's ashes. Mummy then shared out some forget-me-not seeds which the vet had given to them. They planted them in a pot to mark the place where Purrfect was buried.

Arin thought it would be nice if they could paint stones to place around the area too.

The children found some smooth stones and took them into the kitchen.

On the table were paint pots and brushes. There was also some orange juice and some chocolate biscuits for everyone.

Arin painted a fish,
because that was
Purrfect's favourite
supper.

Bala painted a
butterfly because
Purrfect loved
chasing butterflies.

Gracie painted a happy
face to remind them of
the happy times they
had all played together.

About the author

Carole was inspired to write this book following a series of events in the lives of her grandchildren. After researching books to support them emotionally through difficult situations she felt inspired to write a book herself. This book differs from other books that deal with life events as it is written in such a way that children can engage with the story at any time, not just when a pet has died. It is an adventure story, with colourful, eye-catching and original illustrations.

This is intended to be the first of a series of books, dealing with a variety of situations which children may experience.

7 7 6

5

4

My → ③
House

2

GRACIE'S

Hedgehog Crescent